THE BLACK FAIRY AND THE DRAGONFLY
ESCAPE FROM THE DARK QUEEN

(BOOK 2)

Copyright © 2014 Paul G Day

CONTENTS

ACKNOWLEDGMENTS

Special thanks to my Editor and friend Janice Spina for her editorial work, encouragement and advice and for taking me on and believing in my work. Her dedication to the work of Indie Authors is tremendous. Thanks also to Chris Graham for is help with this book.

Finally, my darling wife. You are a constant source of support for me personally and I love you very much. Thank you for understanding me and allowing me to go on this incredible adventure. I owe you everything.

PRAISE FOR THE BLACK FAIRY AND THE DRAGONFLY

"If you're a fan of George MacDonald's work, or Andrew Lang's rainbow of Fairy Books, you'll enjoy this story. It's perfect for a read-aloud, for listeners ranging from 3 to 7, with short chapters that keep the story moving."
(The Kindle Book review)

"My granddaughter loved it so much I had to read it to her every day she was at my house, she now plays like she is Lilly"
(D Boydston)

"Quite an unusual story, but a very quick and enjoyable read, clean and nothing too gory. This little fairy tale is more for a younger reader, but I enjoyed it considerably" (Ms Marzipan)

"An enchanting tale that captures the imagination and takes you on a fantastic voyage of discovery, adventure, friendship and courage" (Cindy Beitinger)

"This is the first book I have read by Paul Day and it will certainly not be the last. This author has a special gift in the way he creates a magical world of fairies for children to travel through." (J Spina)

"This book grabbed my interest the whole entire time. Not many books can do that." (Maddie P)

PROLOGUE: TOO SMALL IS HER SHOULDER

Lilly remembered well the feelings of loneliness and isolation in the months and years she had spent on the edge of the Fairy Kingdom. She remembered also the terrible sadness after her parents passed into the realm of fairy ghosts. The Elders had banished her, for reasons she could not fathom.

"We cannot afford to trust that the same thing won't happen to other fairies, that they too won't be orphaned by some strange and dreadful curse," they had said.

They had not blamed her directly, but Lilly knew it by the way their mouths formed the words and by the way their eyes avoided hers and by the insight deep inside her ever-thinking mind. She read it in the tone of their voices and in their posture as well. "If the body of a fairy has its own language, then theirs was loud and clear", said Lilly often to herself, "You are responsible for their deaths."

It was a troubling thought that soon became a truth in her heart, so that Lilly started to believe herself that it was her fault. After all, everything that had happened to her and her family was terrible. Then, when the fairies themselves disappeared and the burden of blame, though undeserved, fell heavy on her tiny shoulders, the weight of it became impossible to bare.

If she had been a stronger being, perhaps an angel or a winged beast of the forest or an eagle, she would surely have been able to carry the load. But as it was, her shoulders were simply too small.

Lilly had often wandered by the waters of the lakes bordering the Kingdom. She had seen the water lilies, with their great petals reaching high into the sunlight. The green, almost petal-shaped leaves under the flower formed boats that fanned out to support them. If you looked at them from high up in a tree, they appeared like stars against the comparative dark of the water. At night, under the light of the full Moon, the thousands of white flowers mirrored the stars of the sky, so that for a while at least, there were two heavens.

Lilly, the dragonflies had named her, when she didn't already have a name. Not because she resembled the Lilies, but because of a small black lily fly which made the flowers its home. The dark lily flies were stark against the stunning white of the flower. And so they named her Lilly Black De-Small.

Oh how she had wished she was as white as a lily or even pale like the daisy. Then none of the trouble she had brought on everyone would have happened. Her parents would still be here. The fairies would never have disappeared. And she would not feel the tremendous guilt she now felt every time she heard their fading songs, night after night in the dreadful dungeons of the Queen.

Paul G Day

CHAPTER 1: A SONG OF CHAINS

The dragonflies were asleep now. Freyse, the one dragonfly who understood Lilly the most, was bobbing his head up and down in jerking movements that at any other time would have made Lilly smile. She had heard him in the night and had thought he called out to her, but when she answered, it became clear to her that he was dreaming.

Lilly herself had been woken by a strange dream. She had found herself in a very long tunnel, at the end of which was a beautiful blue ball of light, surrounded with what appeared to be a halo of white. The ball of light had called to her and she had obeyed. But after walking through the tunnel for a very long time, she seemed no closer to the light.

The tunnel had widened and Lilly felt suddenly very cold. Above her the top of the tunnel had opened up to reveal the brilliant stars that spun and flickered far above. Ahead of her the strange blue sphere called to her again and this time there was no mistaking the sound.

L-I-L-L-Y.

She had dreamed about the crystal sphere before, but something had changed. The voice grew more and more urgent as it echoed throughout the chasm. An icicle must have fallen from somewhere above, for it crashed loudly to the icy floor and splintered into a thousand shards of ice, each one clanging and clinking off of each other, as they danced about the floor seemingly in slow motion.

The cacophony of sounds found their way to the other end of the chasm and the blue sphere instantly reacted, suddenly filling the chasm with an iridescent light that reflected off everything around about. Lilly had to shut her eyes for a moment because the light was so brilliant. But when she opened them again, the crystal sphere was silent and dim.

She was drawn to it. It seemed so familiar to her now. What had once appeared only in her dreams, was now very much in her heart. She had spoken to it and it had answered. She was even able to ask it questions, but the answers were not easy to understand and came to her as if a multitude of fairy children were all talking at once.

Finally, she drew so close to the sphere that had she taken but a few more steps, she might very well have been able to touch it. But she dared not. She trusted it. It had not harmed her in her dreams. It had given her a warmth that, Despite the icy cold of the chasm, had somehow made her feel at ease.

But on this particular night and in this particular dream, something happened that Lilly could not have anticipated. She heard, as if she were standing right there in the chasm, the unmistakable voice of someone she loved. Someone she had missed so badly. Someone she used to call her mother.

Through the tears forming in her dreamy eyes, Lilly strained to make out the shape and form inside the sphere. Every time she had seen it, there were so many forms, dancing around inside, like the shadows of creatures she once recognized but now could not. All other forms were still. Only one form grew large inside the sphere until it filled almost the entire thing.

When she recognized the shape of the being right there in front of her, she instinctively ran to it and then had to stop herself for fear of what might happen if she touched the blue light. It wasn't that she was afraid, she had showed great courage before. It wasn't that she was timid, she was anything but that. It was just this tiny little voice inside her heart that she had ignored once before and was captured by the Queen as a result. A voice that said *careful*.

The shape was still blurred, mixed as it was with the colors and shapes beyond it. She stood still and gazed hopefully into the white eyes now forming and then she heard it again.

"My Lilly."

Then she had woken to the sound of singing. She sat up on the cold, stone floor of her cage and noticed that all three dragonflies were awake and staring at her.

"We thought you had died," said Skeye, his head cocked to the side.

"Yes, yes, dead," agreed Leafel, who had his head firmly wedged into the bars of their cage. "But not dead, not ever dead, not now, at least not now, not ever dead."

Freyes had noted a tear that had stubbornly clung to Lilly's chin and he reached through the bars with his hairy foot and gently wiped it away. That act of kindness brought a welcome smile from Lilly.

"No, not dead. Just sad, so very sad, always so sad." He said.

Lilly had not loved anyone since losing her parents. The gentleness of Freyes brought an image of the shape of her mother in the dream. She had to fight back a new tear replacing the old one. But there was no time for it now. She turned her head and squeezed her eyes shut and tried to picture the fairy ponds and lakes back home. *This is why I am here*, she thought as she listened to the songs still so far away.

Each night and every morning the fairies had sung their songs, much to the annoyance of the Roaches that the Queen had placed as guards. A long time ago, Lilly had not met a single creature she did not like. Beetles, bees, grasshoppers, ants and even wasps. They had never harmed her and had only ever been kind. Through the forests and lands of the Fairy

Kingdom, Lilly herself had become legend, mostly without her knowledge and certainly without her permission. Freyes had told her so himself late one night as she lay sleepless on the stone. He had wanted to cheer her up by telling her stories. He was not very good at it, but she had neither the heart, nor the inclination to tell him so. She was just glad that he was there.

"Black Princess they call you."

"Little Dark Angel," added Leafel.

"Yes, Princess and Angel, all over the Kingdoms, all over the world, yes that's what they say," Skeye chimed in.

"All the insects and furry creatures, even the great sea birds. They all know your name. Yes all. Even all the creatures in the mountains." Said Freyes, as he cocked his head proudly. "My Lilly. Our Lilly. Oh Lilly, you could never die. Not now, not ever."

"But how do you know all this?" Lilly asked innocently.

"Oh we know. Dragonflies know," answered Leafel.

"Oh yes, we know. Of course we know. We know all, we see all, we hear all," added Skeye.

"Whispered on the air, from near and far it is. Come straight to small ears through cages nearby. Then carried to us from voices so small. So very small," Freyes explained.

"I still don't understand," Lilly said.

"Look, see. So small. So very small."

Freyes had turned his back towards Lilly. On his back was the smallest creature she had ever seen. She had to step closer as it was difficult to see in the dim fire lit dark of the dungeon. But there, sure enough was a flea. Of course Lilly had seen fleas before, though there weren't many in the fairy Kingdom. But Sparrows and other birds had fleas, as did rodents and all furry creatures.

"It speaks to you?" said Lilly, more than a little flabbergasted.

"Oh, yes, talks and talks and talks," answered Freyes.

"Oh yes they can talk. Can talk up a storm. They never stop talking. It's all they ever do. It's all they can do. Oh that and jump very high," said Skeye.

"Too much in fact. Too much they say. So much and so often. Too long and too fast. They don't slow down, not ever," added Leafel.

"Shhhh!" whispered Lilly abruptly as she noticed a Roach coming their way. Yes she had never disliked any creature, until she met the roaches. "A roach is coming."

"You. You and you and you and even you. Keep to yourself and stop that chatter. Right? Got it? Got it good and proper?"

With that the Roach turned and went back to his position guarding the main door.

"I don't like roaches," said Leafel. So mean. So very mean.

"That makes four of us," said Lilly. Then she turned to Freyes and beamed a big smile at him. "So, these fleas. They speak as you do?"

"Oh yes, yes of course and even as you do."

"You mean they can speak other languages?"

"Yes, indeed yes. Any and all, in fact, every language," answered Skeye excitedly, as if he himself was just beginning to understand what he just said.

Lilly had never thought to talk to a flea. She had met so few of them that it had never once crossed her mind that they even had a language, let alone could talk. Even if she had known, she would never have heard one, unless it was close enough to climb up on her shoulder and speak straight into her ear.

So this revelation was astounding. As astounding as any bit of knowledge she ever heard before. Not only that but extremely useful as well.

At the other end of the dungeon, the distant fairies were still singing, but it was a solemn song they now sung. After that first song, the song that made Lilly realize she had found the lost fairies, the songs had become more and more subdued. The fairies had taken to using anything around them as instruments in an effort to give their songs more volume. Tin cups, bits of bone, even their chains were used. They had become quite clever at their use too. Who knew chains and bones and cups could be used to make such beautiful music. But then, fairies were renowned for their music and fashioning instruments was learned from a young age.

As Lilly sat and listened to their singing and the music of the sound of the fairies' chains, an idea began to form from a single thought, which then sprouted into a complete image, which then formed a vision in her mind. But it was late in the night before Lilly had the answer to a great puzzle she had been thinking about ever since she woke up for the first time in the dungeon.

The dragonflies had given her the knowledge about the most unlikely of little creatures and their habit of learning the language of all others. Now one of those creatures was whispering in the ear of Freyes, who seemed to have stopped listening a while ago.

"Freyes, can I borrow the little chatter box for a moment?" Freyes seemed to guess what she was up to, but Skeye and Leafel cocked their heads in a manner which seemed to suggest they didn't have a clue.

The flea did not wait for Freyes, but hopped down from his back and jumped across the floor and leaped up onto Lilly's shoulder. Then it positioned itself close to her ear and told her what she had already guessed.

A wide smile from Lilly was all Freyes needed. He nodded in her direction. Leafel and Skeye began nodding as well, as they slowly worked out what was going on…

The Dungeons of Eglarth

Chapter 2

CHAPTER 2: THE DUNGEON OF EGLARTH

Flick, that's what his name was. Such a curious little creature. Lively, quick and with a personality all his own. So happy he was, listening to Lilly as he sat there on her shoulder, his head flicking left and right, his little antennae vibrating as it curled towards her. When he spoke, he rushed through his words like a squirrel chomps through an acorn as if it was the last acorn in the world.

He had lived in the dungeon all his short life and had known no other home. So when Lilly told him all about the forests, the rich green trees, the huge flowers, the giant mushrooms and the lakes that stretched out to the horizon, he was as quiet as a little flea knew how to be. When he interrupted Lilly she rebuked him. "Now just wait, little flea they call Flick. I haven't finished yet." He seemed impatient. Lilly knew he was eager to tell her all about the dungeon and the rats and the habits of the roaches and other creatures that lurked in the dark.

When she was finished, he told her about the rats and other rodents and how they were misunderstood by all other creatures. He told her that without them, the fleas would have no home. He told her that the rats provided a home in their fur and in return the fleas made sure the rats knew where all the best food was, discarded fruit, nut shells, snails and slugs and other slimy creatures. Lilly did not want to know about any of that. She struggled to imagine any creature devouring such things.

He told her that the roaches were simple creatures who never questioned the Queen. She only had to give them orders and they obeyed without thinking, never once arguing with her. He told her that their shells were hard and that they fought amongst themselves for the scraps that came from the Queen's kitchens.

Lilly listened intently to everything the little flea told her. In her mind and in her heart, a plan was beginning to take shape. She had wondered on those cold sleepless nights, so many nights since they were captured, about how they would escape, about how they would free the other fairies. But most of all, she was desperate to know what the Queen wanted of them all. For that the flea had no answer and troubled thoughts made Lilly shiver.

After listening to the flea for a long time, she asked Flick what he knew of the habits of the Queen. "She comes here. Not often, but she does come. She is dark. So very dark. She has great power. She casts spells on little creatures without provocation. She turns little creatures into stone, into bone, into anything she likes," he said. "Then, when she has tormented them enough, she places them in small jars and puts them on display for the entertainment of her minions."

"Minions," asked Lilly, interrupting him.

"Oh yes, minions. Hard to describe they are. Hairy, short and fat, with sharp teeth and a ferocious appetite. Will eat anything, they will."

Lilly thought about the banquet at the Queen's table and about the strange creatures under the spells of the Queen. So many strange creatures, unlike any she had ever seen. Some tall and skinny, some short and fat. Some with dark skin and some with brown hair. Many of them had horns on their heads and their garments were dull and dreary. They laughed when the Queen laughed, sang when she commanded and yet they played music such as Lilly had never heard before. Music which mesmerized her as she watched them play and dance and entertain. But she had forgotten about them after being captured. So much of her energy had since been used up thinking about their plight.

"They weren't always like that," added Flick.

"What do you mean?" replied Lilly.

"They were different before, when she captured them. They were, as you would call them, creatures from the other world. Your world."

My world. Lilly allowed the thought to take root in her being. She thought about the creatures of the forest. Rabbits, squirrels, foxes, birds and many more besides. Then it occurred to her that when she and Freyes went to look for the fairies, she had not seen a single other creature in the forest. She didn't know why she hadn't noticed before. Maybe she was so focused on finding the fairies, she did not have space in her heart to wonder about the other creatures.

"You mean from the Fairy Kingdom? The creatures are all from home?" she said, finally.

"Yes, yes I think so. I saw them come in, just like you. Fur of white and some like mustard, shimmering wings, soft and delicate and very afraid. But then—" Flick stopped mid sentence.

"But then what?" Lilly said, a puzzled look on her face. She already knew what he was about to say. The little voice in her heart had told her.

"In the dungeon of the Queen, strange magic takes place. Creatures that were once beautiful and full of color, change, in time...eventually, I mean."

Lilly got up and walked over to the iron bars separating her from the dragonflies. They were fast asleep. She did not realize that she and Flick had talked for so long. She looked at Skeye and Leafel and her dear friend Freyes. She tried to imagine them changing into something…something dreadful, but she could not.

"This cannot happen. It simply cannot."

She thought about the fairies and the forests and lakes back home. She thought about the wide world above them and how sad a place it would be if all the creatures of the world were captured and brought to this dreadful place. She thought about the Elders and how regretful they must be. She thought about all the future fairies that would never be born. She remembered the dreams she had had about the crystal sphere and how she had seen and heard her mother call to her. The sphere seemed intent on finding Lilly. It seemed to want to tell her something. But she knew not what that something was.

Lilly closed her eyes and tried hard to remember the songs her mother had taught her and the enchantments of the magic she had learned. Then she recalled the moment she freed herself and the dragonflies from Denheroth. The Queen had seemed genuinely amazed that such a small creature had such strange powers.

But nothing she had tried had worked on the Queen. She was simply too powerful. No magic Lilly possessed was strong enough to release them from the chains that bound their hands and necks and feet.

Suddenly, as Lilly thought about everything, there was a commotion beyond the cages. The roaches, that had always stood guard, quickly scurried off through a large, heavy wooden door. In the distance Lilly heard a dreadful, now familiar sound and she knew, oh how her little heart knew, the Queen had returned.

Escape From The Dark Queen

Chapter 3

CHAPTER 3 ESCAPE FROM THE DARK QUEEN

The dragonflies greeted Lilly's plan with excited clicking and twitching and humming. She had not seen them so happy in ages. They had been so fearful when the Queen came into the dungeon. She had knelt down and peered into their cages, her fiery eyes blazing with a mixture of curiosity and fury.

A hapless rodent had made the terrible mistake of crossing her path as she strode towards the cages and she flicked a hand in its direction and it was instantly turned to skeleton, frozen right there on the spot. She had kicked it away with a foot and it smashed against a wall, broken bones scattering in all directions.

Flick had seen it and a tiny voice squealed in Lilly's ear. Flick had spent many hours on her shoulder and the two of them had become almost inseparable. She felt the little creature trembling as it snuggled into the crest of her ear. Now she had a new reason to escape. Not that she needed any more reasons. Since she had found the fairies, she had also learned of the fate of many of the creatures from the forest. More and more creatures in the world, it seemed, were depending on her for rescue, whether they knew it or not.

As for the dragonflies, they huddled in the corner of their cage. Freyes had his wings spread wide to protect Leafel and Skeye. Lilly had marveled at his growing bravery and she knew he was becoming every bit the leader that Vanos had expected him to be.

"Such a curious little creature, aren't you my little black thing," the Queen had said menacingly as she peered between the bars. "Tell me, how strong is your magic? Strong enough to rescue yourself? Maybe." She added, as if in answer to her own question. "Yes, maybe. But tell me this little dark angel, isn't that what they call you now? Tell me, can you rescue the other fairies?"

Lilly tried so very hard to not show the fear she was feeling inside. In her heart, she felt a sudden urge to flee. But to where and how. But on her face, she showed the determination and resilience her parents had taught her. *Be strong Lilly*, she almost heard her mother saying. She wondered if the Queen could see into her mind and deep inside her heart. She wondered what other secrets the Queen had learned about her.

"Only the most courageous and powerful creature would ever dare try to escape this place. There would be a world of trouble for such as she." The Queen used her terrible charms, that swung and glowed from her neck. The force of her magic pulled Lilly towards the bars. Try as she might, she was unable to escape it. Lilly was now standing at the bars, a breath away from the face of the Queen. She felt a sweet, intoxicating smell coming from the mouth that loomed like a large red rose, opening and closing as the Queen spoke her magic, her white teeth like jewels lining the top and bottom of a dark, red cave.

Lilly was almost overcome. She had to use her own magic to ward off the influence of the Queen as the Queen herself searched Lilly's heart, opening up the memories locked inside, only for Lilly to at last close them with her own magic.

The Queen looked suddenly angry and pulled herself up. Her shadow cast itself over everything. Her eyes were now wild and wide.

An aura surrounded her. It changed color from the deep blue to emerald and scarlet. The Queen hissed and then leant forward and with a booming voice she filled the chamber with sound.

"SO, BLACK ANGEL. YOU WANT TO PLAY GAMES. USE YOUR MAGIC IF YOU MUST. IT MATTERS LITTLE."

Then the Queen softened her voice and took on a whole new tone. At first Lilly did not know what to make of it. "My Lilly. My dear, sweet Lilly." She said in a voice like that of Lilly's dream. Then she roared with laughter. The minions who stood at a distance behind her laughed with her, mocking Lilly with their raucous, scornful noise.

As the Queen left the chamber, Lilly feared that the Queen truly could see into her heart. How else would she have known about her dreams. She shivered again as she realized that she now had little time left. The Queen had given no clue what she wanted from Lilly and she was not about to stay and find out.

"The time is right." She said to the dragonflies after a few moments, when the air had once more fallen silent. In the distance the fairies had struck up another song. They must surely have heard the Queen and were afraid. But it had not stopped them from singing. They now sang with full voice, filling the air with a more welcome sound.

Lilly spoke to Flick briefly and he hopped down and away through the bars and into the shadows. He returned after a while with news Lilly desperately wanted to hear.

"They have agreed. Yes indeed. They have agreed."

It brought a rare smile to Lilly's face and warmth once more filled her being. She watched the roaches, who had returned to their stations and waited for the signal. She looked closely at the key chain dangling from a large hook to the side of the main doorway. It was big. She had not yet worked out how she would manage it, but there was no time to worry. She would have to jump that lily pad when it came time.

The attention of the roaches was drawn away to the sound of a multitude of clawed feet scurrying towards them from a way off. Perhaps, if the roaches had not opened the door to see what was coming, Lilly's plan would have been thwarted. Perhaps if they weren't such simple creatures, they might have thought before acting. But being roaches, she forgave them their stupidity and was glad for it.

So when they opened the door, they were met by the force of a hundred rodents, all scrambling over each other and bringing the roaches crashing to the floor. They did not stand a chance. The rodents, led by a few large rats, continued on down the long corridor in the direction of the other fairies, deep into the shadows and disappeared. But their excited screeching and squealing could be heard over the singing of the fairies.

All of them, all together, like a wave of fur. All, that is, except for one. A rat was leaning up against the wall, leaping occasionally to reach the keys. It took a few tries, but at last it knocked the keys off the hook and grabbed them firmly between its teeth. As if obeying an invisible command, the rat then brought the key over to Lilly's cage and dropped them at the bars. But when Lilly tried to lift them, she could not. She called out to Flick who was hidden in the fur inside the ear of the rat.

"Tell him to pick up the keys and open the lock."

The rat seemed confused for a moment, looking first at Lilly and then back at the keys. For the briefest of moments, Lilly thought the rat would not or could not do it. She wasn't sure if a rat even knew what keys were, let alone how to use them. But to her surprise, eventually the rat must have understood what Flick was telling it to do and it grabbed the keys with a claw and wrestled it into the lock.

In the distance Lilly heard what sounded like marching. The sound was joined by another, more terrible noise. She hoped the noise was much further away than it sounded. Behind her the dragonflies were flicking about excitedly. She heard Freyes calling out to her, but she couldn't hear what he was saying with all the other noises echoing throughout the dungeon.

It took such a long time, but over the din, Lilly heard the most beautiful sound she thought she would never hear. With a snap and a click the large padlock came undone and a chain smacked hard to the floor. The rat pulled the large iron door open and Lilly flew out of her cage.

With no time to bask in her new found freedom, she commanded Flick to open the other cages and she flew off into the dark of the corridor, following the sounds of singing, which sounded to Lilly much more energized than before. Through a maze of hallways, she flew first round one corner, then another and another until, at the end of one last corridor, she saw them.

At the bars of the imprisoned fairies, she was greeted with an excited chorus of cheer. One of the elders, who was pressing hard up against the bars, with a tear in his aging eyes, greeted Lilly with words she had never dared dream she would hear.

"So sorry Lilly. So sorry for all this trouble. So sorry about abandoning you in your need. So terribly sorry." She took a fraction of a moment to look into his eyes and see his heart. Inside he was no different to any other fairy. It was fear that had driven Lilly away, she had decided. Fear of the unknown. Fear of dark magic. However misplaced that fear was, it was innocent. Lilly had often thought about what she would say to the elders, how she would rebuke them. How she would shame them for what they had done to her and her parents. But in that moment, seeing the fear in the eyes of a fairy elder, she forgave him. She forgave them all.

Behind her, Lilly heard the Queen, barking loudly at the roaches, cursing them to get out of her way. A great burst of light filled the adjacent corridor and Lilly knew they had no time left.

She ordered the fairies to follow the rodents out of the dungeon and told Leafel and Skeye to follow. But she and Freyes stayed right where they were. She needed time. Time is all she wanted and time is all she needed. Any time, no matter how small, no matter how long or even how short.

As the Queen closed in and the fairies disappeared out through one last door and to their freedom, Lilly stood firm, with Freyes above and behind her. She caught sight of another shadow and looked over to see the elder standing right beside her. He held a staff in his hand. A staff she had thought was used only to carry him along when walking. A simple staff made of wood from the Forest Elm. But in the cleft of a claw carved in the top of the staff was a charm. From where it came, Lilly did not know. She had not seen it before. She did not remember the fairy elders ever having charms.

The elder gave Lilly a knowing nod and then winked. As the Queen came around the corner, preceded by a flash of orange light, the two fairies, together with the dragonfly, stood their ground.

"YOU THINK YOU CAN OUTPLAY ME? ME, QUEEN EGLARTHARIOUS? QUEEN OF THE UNDERWORLD, OF THE LIVING AND THE DEAD?"

The sound of her voice was like the rolling of thunder as it cracked and blew towards them. Then the Queen raised her dreadful hands, as her black wings unfurled behind her. Lilly raised her own hands outward and, with all her power, with all her magic, with all her heart, she used every song, every spell, all mixed in together and shouted them out at the Queen.

She didn't know it then, but beside her, the elder had his staff outstretched. He had convinced the Queen he needed the staff to walk and foolishly she had let him.

Suddenly there was a burst of blue light that came from behind and around them. So powerful was the light it knocked the queen backwards and sent her crashing into the roaches positioned behind her. It sent them so fast that some of the roaches were squashed against the wall. When Lilly opened her eyes and looked, the Queen was struggling on the floor. Blue lightning was zapping around her and she was screaming in agony.

Lilly felt a hand grab her and the three of them, Lilly, the fairy elder and Freyes, flew down the corridor and out through the last great door.

Outside they were met with rejoicing and singing. Lilly acted quickly and told them there was no time to celebrate.

"We must leave now. We must go." She said sternly.

"Yes, leave we must. Go we must. Now, if possible, even now," said Freyes.

Lilly had no time. Time is all she needed. But there simply was none, never enough. She didn't have time to rejoice. She didn't have time to smile. There was no time to hug, no time to linger. She didn't even have time to check, to see for certain, to see if the Queen was dead. Oh she wanted her dead. It was her one terrible wish. Not because she hated her, nor because she liked death, but to keep the fairies safe, to keep the world from harm, to keep all the creatures of all the world beyond the clutches of evil, now and forever.

Lilly had freed the fairies. She, along with the dragonflies and because of a tiny little flea, had succeeded. But now there was a new course. The minions, creatures that once called the forests of the kingdom of fairies home. They were still back there in the dungeon of the Queen.

So as she fled with the fairies, in her heart of hearts, Lilly made a simple little promise.

"I will set you free."

The Frog Lords of Sereth-Ebon

Chapter 4

CHAPTER 4 THE FROG LORDS OF SERETH-EBON

Deep inside every creature who has ever lived, lies a great mystery. This mystery finds form in the shape of the life each creature lives and the lessons they have learned. It's a certain kind of magic to know that it exists and even greater comfort to those who are alone. It is what drove Lilly for all this time. It's what gave her courage when it was most needed. It was what helped her overcome the Queen against impossible odds.

But now Lilly was no longer alone. Instead she found herself surrounded by fairies again. Only this time, she was welcomed as one of them once more. So small, so very black and unassuming as she was, Lilly was glad for one thing. She had company. Yes she had lived among the dragonflies. They had given her a name. They had made her part of their clan. But to be here, with the fairies, though still far from home, was far more than she could possibly have hoped for. Instead of the outcast she was their hero, their Lilly. And not just theirs either, for her fame had spread far away to distant lands. To the shores of the great oceans, to the great impenetrable forests inland and even all the way high up in the Mystical Mountains, where snow as deep as the trees are high, covers their peaks all year round.

Rumors of the legend of this tiny creature reached the ears of the ancients who inhabit the ice castles on the sides of the mountains. The legends were carried by fleas, who whispered them to sparrows, who in turn told her story to gulls and finally to the crested Eagles of the mountains, who, because they had a unique relationship with the ancients, brought word of her fame to their ears.

So it was no surprise that the fairies were visited by a messenger. What was surprising was the message.

"We, the creatures of the Mystical Mountains, have heard the wonders of your story. We send you this messenger to tell you that everything you have ever done, thought or felt, has been noted. It won't be long now till you fulfill your destiny. It won't be long now till your dreams come true."

This message of great import was well received by the fairies, who had settled in the marshes of the Frog Lords, far away from the underworld.

After their escape from the Dark Queen, Freyes, Skye and Leafel returned to the dragonfly kingdom to give a report to Vanos. Vanos himself had grown gravely ill and they reached him just in time. Their report gave him much cheer, but he was far too old now and he passed into the realm of dragonfly ghosts.

When her three companions returned, they came with a thousand other dragonflies to take the fairies home, to live for a while with them. But when Lilly learned that Vanos had passed away, she was overcome with grief and nobody could comfort her for many days.

As time passed, she realized with regret that the time had come to say her goodbyes. The fairies mounted, each one their dragonfly, with the little ones in baskets woven from river reeds, which were slung behind the neck of the dragonflies and strapped down tight for the journey home. Only she and two of the elders, along with the three dragonflies she trusted the most, remained behind to solve a great mystery.

The fairies, though reluctant to leave their champion Lilly, nevertheless left on the great wings of these, the largest of all insects she had known in the world and headed off into the clouds. As Lilly waved one final wave, as the last of the dragonflies disappeared into the silvery clouds, a tear formed on her cheek. So many tears these days and so often. So much to grieve for, so much pain and yet, also, so much joy and relief.

Lilly did not yet know what had become of the Queen. She could not hope so much that they would never see her again. That little voice that so often spoke quietly in her heart, had given her good reason to doubt the Queen was dead.

As for the Frog Lords. Their world sat between the underworld and the Mountains to the North. They, along with the Horned Beetles and other creatures, were all that remained. They assured Lilly that they had skill and armies enough to overcome or at least delay the Queen, should she chance appearing from her eternal underworld kingdom and venture into the world above.

Snorl, the King of the Frog Lords was a large, blubbering creature, with a mouth as big as a rat and a tongue as long as the neck of a stork. But he had a heart of precious stone and was eager to please the fairies. In the short time the fairies had spent with them, the frogs and toads of the marshes, had learned of their adventures. But preceding Lilly always these days, was her legend.

When they arrived, tired and hungry in their relentless flight from the underworld, the Frog Lords welcomed them, introducing themselves one by one to Lilly as if she were royalty, as if she were a Queen herself. Lilly had never met a Queen, other than Eglartharious. She decided that she wanted no part of it. But when the Frog Lords told her about Sheebas, the beautiful Queen of Grasshoppers, Lilly was intrigued.

Sheebas herself had legends told about her. The Frog Lords even sang songs about her. It was said that she commands legions of grasshoppers and that when they fly on mass the heavens darken and their shadow turns day into night. "Because there are so many," Snorl had said, "no kingdom in all the world dare challenge them. It's just as well they are a peaceful race, or the world would have been overrun an age ago."

Then, when Lilly told the Frog Lords of Eglartharious, they insisted on sending her to meet Sheebas. So, one fine late autumn day, Freyes, Leafel and Skeye had flown all day, until well into the evening to meet her.

Paul G Day

The Dance of The Grasshopper Queen

Chapter 5

CHAPTER 5 THE DANCE OF THE GRASSHOPPER QUEEN

When Lilly finally met the Grasshopper Queen, she was amazed at her beauty. Not like the beauty of a fairy queen, but a unique kind of beauty, such as a little fairy had never seen. She was adorned with fine garments, sewn into the shoulders of her wings and when she flew, her grace and beauty were even more stunning. She was perched high up on a thorny crown, itself draped in all kinds of colorful reeds and flowers.

Lilly bowed low before her. But to her surprise, the Queen flew down and using her front foot, gently raised Lilly back to her feet.

"Oh no," she said. "Never bow. Not now, not today, not even yesterday. Not here, not ever."

Lilly was equally surprised to learn that Grasshoppers and Dragonflies share a similar heritage, speak a similar language and have many things in common. So it was not hard to understand their language. Even their manner, the way they ceaselessly cocked their heads this way and that, their tendency to repeat themselves, it was all very familiar and Lilly felt very much at home.

"Thank you Queen Sheebas, um, your majesty," Lilly said, not even sure if they were the right words.

"My name is Sheeaniasothentantial Norbas The Seventh. But you my dear can call me anything you like. Anything at all."

"Is it ok if I just call you Sheebas, your majesty?"

"Sheebas will do. Yes that will do fine. Very fine indeed. Now come along. Yes come this way along. So much to show you. So much to tell. So much I want to hear as well."

So Lilly had spent many hours with Sheebas, talking, listening to her stories. She was always courteous, always friendly and always very polite. Such a strange distance between this Queen and the other. Lilly never guessed that Queens could be so different. She had never met a Queen Bee, nor the Queen of Ants. She had heard stories about the Queen of Wasps, but they were, all of them, just stories until now. Now Lilly had met a real Queen and what a Queen she was.

The Queen then held a great feast to honor Lilly and all the fairies she had rescued. It was to be a splendid event, but Lilly was only sad that the rest of the fairies could not join them. Then, in the middle of the feast, the Queen did something quite unexpected and very unusual, she left her perch and made her way to the middle of an expanse of dirt, where she started to dance a dance that took Lilly's breath away, such was its beauty. While she danced and kicked and swirled and flicked, beating her wings, making dust fly high into the night sky, other grasshoppers played notes on horns they had borrowed from the kingdom of beetles.

Each one had his or her own horn and they all had a particular note. But when played together, it was as if all the creatures sang in unison together the most magnificent choral song.

The dance went on well into the night. The Queen was joined by others and Lilly could not resist joining in. Even her dragonfly companions gave it a go, though their's was much more clumsy a dance. But she didn't have the heart to tell them, seeing they had so much fun.

The next morning, gifts were brought to Lilly and she was given the use of worker beetles to carry the gifts, plus food and juices in pine bottles.

"You will need all this for your travels." Said the Queen.

Lilly had told Sheebas about her strange dreams, about her mother and her father and about the vision of the crystal sphere. Sheebas herself had great knowledge. She knew about the dragonfly kingdom. She knew about the Beetle King and his armies of beetles. She knew about the Hills of Dancing Fire. She even knew about the mountain creatures, as well as the legendary hanging gardens of ice crystals. "Such stories I could tell you. So many stories. Even as many as there is no time. Stories of the great, stories of the small and even stories in between them all."

While Lilly sat listening to the Queen, she thought about all those creatures still trapped in the dungeons of Eglartharious. She waited patiently for Sheebas to finish. Then, when she had only a moment to interrupt, she took that moment.

"Your majesty, Queen Sheebas. I have to tell you something. Something very important, something even very grave."

"What is it my child, what is it my dear. Quick, tell me little angel, yes tell me, never fear."

"There are creatures, hundreds of them, even thousands, perhaps more, all in danger, all trapped in the dungeons of Eglarth." She said, trying to not sound too dramatic.

"Oh goodness dear. Oh goodness me. That is grave, that is even serious. Oh goodness tell me more."

So she told the Queen all about it, leaving no detail unsaid. She even chanced to tell Sheebas about her own special magic and the power she possessed. When she had finished, the Queen was silent for the first time since Lilly had met her. She turned, paced, cocked her head and paced about some more. Seeing her do this reminded Lilly of Vanos. How similar they were. He a King and she a Queen. So similar and yet so different. Finally Sheebas stopped pacing and turned to Lilly.

"You must go to the Mystical Mountains. You must find the creatures that dwell there. You must not stop. You must go tomorrow, in the morn. Yes, you must go tomorrow, even tomorrow at dawn."

CHAPTER 6: THE MYSTICAL MOUNTAINS

With the fairies now safely back in the forests of the fairy kingdom, where they belonged, Lilly led her small band of companions North from the world of Frog Lords and the Kingdom of Horned Beetles and the safety of the beautiful Grasshopper Queen.

Leafel, Skye and Freyes carried the little fairy and the two fairy Elders on their backs for the long journey. They flew during the day and rested high up in the pines at night. The days were growing short and the nights long and bitterly cold. The dragonflies were not accustomed to the icy cold of the northern lands and Lilly knew the mountains would test them. Being dragonflies, they were used to the warm, tropical climate of the marshes and lakes and jungles of their home. But her dragonflies did not complain.

Freyes had his staff, given to him by Vanos all those months ago. Behind them, the horned beetles that Sheebas had given them struggled with their heavy bodies and small wings, but they were determined to keep up, though progress was slower than it had been before.

Lilly had once heard Sheebas describe the beetles as the mules of the sky. They were strong, resilient and could carry far greater loads than the dragonflies ever could. Their wings made a low pitched buzzing sound similar to the bumble bees of the forests. Over the relentless cold winds, the noise was a constant presence and became something of a comfort to her.

In her heart, Lilly wondered what strange magic had brought her growing clan of loyal travelers together. Such an unlikely group of companions there never was, but Lilly was more than grateful for their company.

As the mountains loomed each day larger and larger ahead of them, Lilly began imagining what new discoveries lay ahead. She had heard of the strange and beautiful creatures that inhabited the mountains. She had met rabbits and foxes and other such creatures a few times in her short life, but no amount of imagining conjured up images she trusted concerning the mystical creatures.

At night, when they were all quietly sleeping high up in the comfort of the pine trees, the few times she was able to sleep, she dreamed. Her dreams were becoming more strange, more vivid, more real, with every passing night. Often, she dreamed of the crystal sphere. She could now understand its voice, but struggled to comprehend the meaning.

"I see you," it said to her, "you draw near. My precious little angel draws so very near. So dear and so very near."

When they finally drew close enough to the mountains, the trees thinned and it was hard to find trees big enough to provide the shelter they needed from the driving wind and falling snows. Lilly herself had learned to control her magic. It was what sustained her on the journey. It gave her warmth at night. So strong was her magic now that she glowed at night and the others huddled close to her, feeding off her warmth.

Every opportunity she had, she tried to remember more of the spells and chants and songs she had been taught so long ago. She recited them in her heart every day and at night, when she couldn't sleep, she practiced them with her inner voice.

"You glow. Yes, you glow," said Freyes one especially cold night.

"Yes, we see it. We feel it. Stronger. Ever stronger. Each night we feel it," added Skye.

Lilly did not know quite what to make of it. Something, she thought. Something about the sphere, about these mountains, about this mysterious and mystical place, was giving her strength and warming her heart.

Finally, they spent one more night in the last pine they could find. Above them the mountains rose so high that they only saw the sunlight for the shortest of time and they seemed to be forever cast in the shadows of the snow covered peaks.

But when she searched the mountain early in the dim morning light, she could see no way up without resting, for there was nowhere to rest.

"I don't know. I just don't know," complained Leafel.

"So big, so vast, so terribly great, these mountains, so high even for dragonflies," added Skeye.

Lilly, seeing they were overcome with doubt, called everyone together. She spoke to the Elders first. She had had so little to do with them when she was young, but as they had spent so many days on this long and dangerous flight, she had become so close to them.

Daniith was the oldest and wisest of them. He was confident and despite his age, was more than capable. It had been he who stood by her side and faced Eglarth. It was he she had learned had questioned the wisdom of the others and had been outvoted when she was only young. He had been so sorry. He had said to her many times, "I am so sorry, my little one. So sorry I did not stand my ground when you were so small."

"But you did. You faced her. You faced the Queen and you stood with me. We would not be here if you had not," she insisted.

"My precious little dark one," he would say. So full of love. So ready to forgive. So strange and wonderful and so very rare indeed."

Lilly had seen a whole new side to the elders. She was beginning to understand their choices, their knowledge of the world and their ways. In her heart she had truly forgiven them. She felt compelled to because of the memory of her parents, especially her mother, who she remembered was always so ready to put the past behind her. Even when she was so ill with grief, her last words, though Lilly was so young, still echoed in her tiny frame.

"You were born for reason, for purpose, for some strange cause. A cause far greater than any anger or disappointment or injustice."

Lilly vowed to honor that memory and the memory of a father who loved her more than life itself. Together, her parents had given Lilly just enough strength, just enough courage and more than enough skill, not only to survive, but to flourish.

"There is a cave, do you see?" said Sethbasish, the second great Elder and life long friend of

Daniith. "Up there in the cleft of a narrow gorge."

Lilly followed his spear as he pointed. At first she could not see it. She followed the gorge with her eyes until finally she saw a small dark shadow, high up at the top.

"I see it. I see it as well, even up there, right there. Up high. I see it," said Skeye.

"Oh yes, high, very high, but not too high. No, not too high at all, not for Leafel," added Leafel.

Freyes had seen it by now as well. They, all six of them stood on a rock beneath the last pine and stared ahead and up into the snowy shadows. The beetles said nothing. It wasn't that they couldn't speak. They couldn't see. Their eyes were not as sharp. They could see only over short distances. Lilly doubted they even saw the mountains until they touched the snow at the base of the largest one.

Then, seeing the small doubt remaining on the faces of her companions, she gathered them together again and searched their hearts.

"We have come so far. Too far in fact for ones so small in a world too big. We have flown over hills dancing with fire that covered everything in every direction. We have met strange and dangerous creatures. We followed the Eagles into a world small creatures are not welcome in. We defeated Denheroth, whose black lightning would have ensnared larger beasts. We escaped the Dark Queen, despite her many charms and great dark magic. We did all this. So to fly up there and rest in that cave is nothing to us."

"You are right," added Freyes, "so very right and so often. We have done all those things, just as you said, all those things and so much more. What is a cave? what is a mountain?"

Lilly did not hesitate, She flew up onto the back of Freyes and Daniith joined her, as he had done every day since they left the kingdom of grasshoppers. Freyes lifted off and then turned to see what the others were doing. He was pleased when he saw them hovering next to him.

Then, with all his strength, with all the power still left in his magnificent, shimmering wings, he took off up the slopes of this mighty mountain. He flew, oh how he soared, with the others not far behind.

The wind howled its disapproval, the large snow flakes beat at them, warning them back, the freezing air dragged at them, determined to pull them down. But still they flew, head on and head long.

The cave, which had seemed so small from way down below, looked large and inviting as they neared the entrance. Huge icicles hung like the teeth of a dragon from the opening and inside, all they could see was a blue-white ice, walls of it on each side and above them. A cool stream flowed below them, coming from deep within.

They flew right inside, deep inside, out of the stinging wind, away from the driving snow and freezing air. They kept flying until they came upon a landing, a great sheet of ice, like a massive floor, made specially for them. They came to rest on the ice, which although it was cold to the touch, was not so cold that it made Lilly shiver. Small puddles formed when she walked on it, melted by the strange warmth her magical body provided.

They found a flat rock in the middle of the shelf of ice. There they rested. The beetles made camp and unloaded the heavy provisions they had carried so far and for so long. They ate, they drank the juice of flowers and then they rested, warm and safe within the cave.

Lilly woke to a strange, new sound. It startled her. She sat up from her bed of petals and peered into the darkness. Beyond the blackness, she saw a distant light, dim, but bright enough that the ice glowed blue around it. She looked around to see everyone else asleep.

For a moment she considered waking the elders, but decided against it. Instead, she hopped up and flew in the direction of the light. But as she approached, the light moved away from her. When she stopped, it also stopped and when she flew it also moved, but always it stayed the same distance. She turned around to see that the others were so far from her that she could barely see them any more. Even though it was dark, the ice itself gave off a hue of white and blue and above them glow worms hung like stars, bespeckling the ceiling of the cave.

Despite her instincts, despite her fear, despite her trembling body and pounding heart, she decided in that moment, that she had to follow the light. Greater than the fear of what she might find, was the fear of losing this one chance forever. She recalled the dreams she often dreamed and how many times she had seen a similar glow from the crystal sphere.

So she followed and followed and followed, deeper and deeper and further inside the massive cave. She flew for so long that she lost track of how long it was. Finally, the blue light stopped and did not move away any more.

Lilly slowly flew on, ducking behind icicles and hiding behind rocks, peering out from behind to see what this light would do. But as she got closer, she heard noises that echoed from ahead and rebounded off the walls around her, softly at first, but growing louder and clearer as she drew closer.

She could now make out some detail in the light, which resembled the ball of light she remembered in her dreams. With trembling hands, she reached down and grabbed a small stone, wrenching it from the ice, which released its grip only after melting away from the stone because of her aura.

She flew up slightly and hovered for a moment. Then she lifted her arm backwards and threw the stone, which hit the ice and clickity clanged, bouncing off rock and ice until it splashed into a stream.

The sphere responded instantly and burst into life. It glowed so bright that it frightened Lilly in the first instance. Then it shimmered and spun and turned, this way, then that, seemingly searching for the sound of the splash. Then, to Lilly's surprise, the sphere mimicked the sound, repeating it over and over until there was a chorus of sound. A thousand splashes echoed throughout the cave so loud and so long that Lilly was sure it would wake the others, even though they were far away.

When the noise abated, Lilly dared fly even closer. Then, with the images of her dreams still fresh in her heart, she drew in a deep breath, closed her eyes and forced her mind to produce an image of her mother, so lovely, so tender, so colorful and so strong. In that moment, every feeling, every memory, every event in her life came flooding back to her, all at once, all together as a powerful, unmistakable image. The image took shape first in her mind and then in her heart and then it filled her soul. Suddenly, everything she had ever thought, had ever wondered, had ever dreamed, came together in one, incredible memory and at last it was all clear, her birth, her purpose, her life. So, when she opened her eyes again she forced out her breath and the breath formed the words she had desperately wanted to say, but could not until this very moment.

"I am here mother."

The Sting of an Angry Hornet

Chapter 7

CHAPTER 7: THE STING OF AN ANGRY HORNET

The Dark Queen used a spell so strong,
A charm of power, a charm of song.
In her cruel dungeon, cold and stark.
There she cast her charms so dark.

A web of fingers the charms brought forth,
With thunder the black lightning roared.
It smacked against the walls so thick,
It was black magic, it was no trick.

Denheroth, in rage did then appear,
But the Queen of darkness did not fear.
For she it was that brought him back,
To chase the fairy, small and black.

After pulling herself up from the dungeon floor and casting all her magic after the little black fairy, Queen Eglarth withdrew to her chambers, still feeling the sting of pain from the combined efforts of Lilly and the Elder.

Her minions escorted her. But they dared not speak. They feared her too much to open their mouths. But deep inside their minds and hearts, after witnessing what one small fairy could do, an even smaller hope grew with just a single thought. The thought was encouraged by a whisper, a little voice inside a willing ear. The voice took shape in the form of a tiny flea. The flea repeated again and again, a word which then became a multitude of silent voices, each one whispering the same thing in the ears of their carriers, the minions. One flea for each of them, one word in each ear.

"Freedom."

When Eglarth finally reached her chambers, she set about making a new potion. She poured into the broth her hatred, her anger and her malice, then added all her darkness together with her fears and all of her bitterness as well.

She clutched her charms, still dangling from her neck with one hand, as she stirred her iron spoon with the other. The brew bubbled and swirled, one dark mix of everything she hated about the world above, filled with everything she knew of the world below. As she stirred, she sang, but it was not like the songs of fairies, so sweet and beautiful, but thunderous and rumbling, like the sound of a thousand stampeding animals of the vast plains of the desert lands.

A dark cloud filled the air above her and spread across the ceiling. Her eyes grew large and red.

Her minions stepped away from her as she grew darker and her eyes grew brighter. When they were back against the wall they huddled together, trembling.

Something came from within the pot, a dark mass, spinning and with it came a terrible noise, a humming, like the buzzing of a thousand bees. It rose as the Queen rose her arms. Then, with the clap of her mighty hands, the spinning dark mass collapsed in on itself and then dispersed into thousands of flying hornets, all with angry yellow eyes. They flew en mass around the chamber, faster and faster, higher and higher until they streamed out through the small window above and were suddenly gone.

Eglarth watched them for a moment as a wide smile appeared on her ever darkening face. Her white teeth shone like the fullest of moons. Her eyes narrowed as beams of orange light cast towards the open window.

"Goodbye my lovelies,
My precious things.
Do your worst,
With your poison stings."

Through the night sky the dark cloud of malice flew swiftly towards the fairy kingdom. Approaching the Mystical Mountains, another dark cloud was slowly making its way towards a cave in the side of the mountain. It knew who it sought, it knew who was in the cave. It needed no Queen to tell it such things. It needed no poison, it needed no light, had no sting in the dark of the night.

Lilly found herself surrounded by darkness. She called out in the black and her own voice returned to her again as an echo.

"Freyes? Leafel? Skeye?" she shouted, as much as a little fairy could shout. But there was no answer but her own.

Suddenly a bright light filled the space around her and a familiar blackness thundered before her, not a few feet away.

"Denheroth?"

The black lightning answered her, but not in a language she understood. It thundered and roared so loudly that she had to cover her ears.

Then another sound filled the space, a strange, deep humming from behind her. But as she was about to turn around to see what new menace was there, Denheroth reached out with his dreadful black fingers and caught her by her arms. She felt herself being pulled by a force greater than her magic. It now held her by her feet and her wings as well.

Then something dark moved around in front of her. It's large yellow eyes met her own. It's wings beat so fast and loud that it was almost as loud as the thunder. *A Hornet*. Thought Lilly as she remembered what Freyes had once said.

"Hornets are not bees. Not like bees at all. Bees are friends of the jungle, friends of the forest. They don't sting. They never sting. But Hornets? Hornets are not friends, no friends at all. They sting. They sting again. Then they sting some more. Always stinging, forever they sting, until after so many stings you don't feel a thing."

The story had made her feel like she never wanted to meet a Hornet. But now one loomed large in front of her, its black body ringed by broad yellow stripes, its large wings gilded with yellow around the edges and deep black veins through transparent gold along the rest. It rose up and presented a red tail, that dripped at its end with a drop of golden liquid, which glowed like a jewel on the tip of its sting.

There was silence, interrupted by laughter from the black lightning. Then Lilly felt the sharp pain of the terrible sting as the Hornet thrust itself deep into her body.

Return to The Chasm of The Crystal Sphere

Chapter 8

CHAPTER 8: RETURN TO THE CHASM OF THE CRYSTAL SPHERE

""Lilly? Lilly" Oh goodness, Lilly. Wake up my Lilly, wake up."

Lilly struggled to open her eyes and when she did it took a few moments to realize where she was. The dream had seemed so real, much more real than any dream she ever had.

"I, I must have fallen asleep," she said, clutching at her stomach where the Hornet in her dream had stung her.

"Yes, yes. Deep sleep, a very deep sleep. So deep was your sleep that we could not wake you. Not wake, never wake." Said Freyes excitedly.

"We thought you were dead. Forever dead. So dead," added Leafel.

"But not our Lilly," said Skeye. "Not dead. Not today, not even tomorrow, not ever dead."

Blue light burst into the cavern and Lilly remembered where she was. The dragonflies and the Elders stood gazing at the incredible light from the Sphere.

"What is it?" said Daniith.

"Everything." Said Lilly as she welcomed the now familiar light. Then, much to the disapproval of the Elders, she got up and approached the sphere and spoke to it. The sphere responded by bursting into a multitude of blues. White shadows streaked around inside it excitedly as she touched the surface with a hand.

"You can speak to it?"

"Oh yes, often."

"And it understands."

"Of course it does."

Suddenly the sphere moved away from Lilly and closer to her companions.

"Daniith. Freyes. Skeye. Leafel and Sethbasish." The blue sphere said, as if it had always been with them.

"It knows our names," said Sethbasish.

"Yes Sethbasish," answered Lilly. "It knows us, because it is us. At least it is who we were meant to be. It is us, our parents, our ancestors, every creature that has ever lived in fact. All of them, their spirits, are in this sphere."

Daniith approached the sphere and it lit up again with delight. He reached out and with his staff he touched it. Immediately it responded with a brilliant show of light and a chorus of sounds rang out and echoed all around the cave. Lilly gave them a reassuring look and then smiled.

"So this is why we came here?" asked Daniith finally? Lilly nodded.

"There are secrets, too many to learn so quickly. The sphere sees all and knows all. But something is coming. Something terrible and strong. Skeye, Freyes, Leafel, we have met him before."

The dragonflies looked bewildered and then a flash of understanding came across them. "Denheroth." Said Freyes. Lilly nodded again.

"The Queen has set a trap."

"The Queen lives?" came the horrified response from Daniith.

"Yes she lives. She has sent Denheroth to intercept us, but she doesn't know I know. But even worse than that, she has sent her hornets to the fairy Kingdom, the dragonfly kingdom and all the kingdoms of the South and West and East. We need to find a way into the Mountains. We need to get help from the mystical creatures. We need to return to our homes before everything is destroyed."

Lilly saw their fear, she felt their hearts, she understood their minds. So great was she becoming, so aware of all around her that there was no longer anything beyond her. With great confidence she spoke to them. She told them of her plans. She was going to deceive the Queen. But to do that, she needed them to be brave and strong. So she told them. She told them everything. She told them the secrets she had learned, the dreams she had. There wasn't anything she kept from them.

Then she sent them, the three dragonflies. She sent them straight, she sent them fast, she sent them on with Vanos' staff.

Then she, along with Daniith and Sethbasish, led by the crystal sphere, headed into the darkness of the mountain. Deeper and deeper and deeper until after going all night, they came out on the other side.

CHAPTER 9 A SPELL OF CHARMS

Lilly had learned much from the Crystal Sphere. It had spoken to her, had sounded so much like her own mother. She even thought she had seen her mother inside. It comforted her to know that she could speak to her. She no longer felt the weight of the whole world upon her tiny shoulders. Instead, she carried with her the knowledge of every life within her heart. It was this knowledge which gave her courage and strength enough to defeat any foe, any power, any dark magic she could possibly meet.

One thing she learned from the Crystal Sphere was that the Queen was not the only one with charms.

When she, Daniith and Sethbasish came out the other side of the Mountain, they were greeted with a dozen wild and wide blue eyes. Lilly did not dare to guess what the Mountain Creatures would be like. She decided it was better simply to see for herself. When she did see them, she decided they were not like any other creatures she had ever seen. They had blue, transparent skin and when they stood in front of light, you could see inside them. Their eyes were bright light blue. They had white hair, each different from the others. Some long to the waist, others short and cropped, some waving about wildly and some straight and still.

In their hands each one carried a bow made of white timbers and carved with ornate carvings. They were embedded with tiny gems and laced with rare metals. They had arrows with large white feathers slung over their shoulders. They were tall and slender and stood above the snow a full length taller than a fox. To Lilly just about everything in the world was bigger. The only thing she had ever met that could speak and was smaller than her was the flea. She had sent Flick on a special errand. He had stayed behind. She knew she would miss him, but it was far more important that he do what was asked of him, so she commanded him to stay.

"For the sake of the creatures now called minions, you must stay. For the sake of the fairies I am sending home you must stay. For the sake of all the creatures that crawl or walk of fly or slither you must stay."

Flick was sad, in the way of a flea, Lilly knew it, but he stayed as commanded to carry out an important task. A task nobody else in the whole world could do. A task for a simple flea and all his kind.

But the creatures of the mountains were so different, so slender, so beautiful, that Lilly found herself staring at them too long on occasions. If only she had known just how exotic she herself was and that these mountain creatures regarded her as the most unusual, interesting and strange of any creature they had ever seen. Yet, it did not take her long to understand them. They did not speak as other creatures did. Their mouths did not move to form words and they rarely showed expressions that differed from the wild, wide-eyed wonder on their faces.

Instead, they seemed able to see into your soul, into your very heart and know without words, without speaking what was on your mind. You could hide nothing from them, so it was pointless trying. Lilly herself had practiced the art of inner sight. Most of the time she was able to tell what her companions were thinking, or at least what they were feeling. So learning to see inside these creatures, did not take her very long.

The creatures were known as Sprites. Not like the green water sprites of the jungle streams, nor like the dessert sprites of the inner lands. These were Ice Sprites and at night they looked for all the world like spirits, their blue bodies glowing with a light that came from the warmth in their white blood. They had pointed ears, so they could hear very well. Their large eyes were perfect for seeing in the dark and they could run on the snow as swiftly and silently as a bird flies on the wind.

After such a long day, Lilly welcomed the rest in a cool ice cave which was surprisingly not as cold as she had expected. Her own inner glow was enough to keep her warm and she snuggled against the bodies of her companions to share her warmth. As she tried to go to sleep, a seemingly endless line of Sprites filed past the cave entrance, all come to see the little black creature called Lilly. They would stare, blinking occasionally in the night, their eyes coming on and off like the dance of fireflies in the fairy forests.

In the morning a very tall Sprite woke her and spoke into her heart. "Come with me little one. Come and see."

Lilly followed the tall Sprite who must have been some kind of elder. Before she did she woke Daniith and Sethbasish. The three of them followed curiously down a series of steps carved into the ice on the side of the cliffs. They then went into a series of caves. Sprites had gathered along the walls of the cave and everywhere all about the caves was bathed in glorious blue light.

They were led through a large carved ice door and into a great room. In the middle of the room was an ice carving, with spires reaching all the way to the ceiling. Every shape imaginable was in the carving, which must have been as large and as grand as the largest trees of the forest.

Crystals of ice hung like beads on vines, swinging away as Lilly and the Elders pushed their way through them. In the center of the carved structure, an old Sprite sat on an ice throne. Lilly knew instinctively she was presented before royalty and she dutifully bowed. The slender creature before her stood up. It wore an ornate gown made of feathers and silk. It had a crystal staff in one hand, with a bright green stone at the top, which shone brightly.

As the King stepped down the steps towards her, it spoke to her heart and she understood. Then the room was filled with bright blue light again as the sphere joined them at his side. A voice came from the sphere and the sound of it sent a wave of emotion through Lilly's entire being.

"Lilly, me dear sweet Lilly. My child. My love. You were always so small, so sweet and so good. We have watched you. We laughed when you laughed, we cried when you cried. We felt your loneliness, your anguish and your pain. We visited you in your dreams in the hope that you would be comforted. Such a small thing to be left all alone so early in life."

Hearing her father's voice brought feelings Lilly had almost forgotten she knew how to feel. A tear flowed freely down one cheek, but froze before it reached her chin. She went to wipe it away but it clung on. She flicked it absentmindedly and it flung away and hit the floor, making a much greater noise than it should. The Crystal Sphere sprung into life in response and a booming voice sprung suddenly from deep within.

"You have been chosen. You were destined for greatness, destined to leave your home. You defeated Denheroth. You stung the Dark Queen. You learned the language of dragonflies and grasshoppers. You met creatures of all sizes, shapes and kinds. You did all this not because you are great, not because you are big, but because your heart has the capacity to be filled with the love of the whole world."

Lilly stood very still, her eyes fixed on the shape inside the sphere, which had grown bigger in the room. Daniith stood beside her, but had stepped back a little. Whether out of fear or respect, Lilly could not tell. In all the times she had heard the voice speak, she had only heard her mother. So to hear her dear father was a shock, but a welcome one.

The sphere went still and shrunk back to its normal size. A dim blue light still filled the space inside the carved structure. The King stood, his eyes wide and bright. He was nodding slowly in Lilly's direction. Another tall sprite stepped towards her. She carried something in her hands. Lilly recognized it as a string of charms, tanzanite charms. They glowed as if they had a light all their own. The sprite stooped to place the charms around the small neck of Lilly. They felt heavier than Lilly had expected, but she soon got used to them. She grasped one of the stones in her hand and examined it.

"What are they?" she asked. The King spoke to her heart again and she understood immediately. "What do I do with them?" Again she was aware of the answer.

When Lilly left the structure, with Daniith and Sethbasish close by her side, they had occasion to ask her what the charms were for. But Lilly did not answer their question, she merely smiled at them for a moment and then said, "Come Elder Daniith, Elder Sethbasish, We have work to do."

The Return of The Lost Fairies

Chapter 10

CHAPTER 10: THE RETURN OF THE LOST FAIRIES

"The Hornets are coming," declared Freyes.

It was early in the morning. A flea had come to him in the night and introduced himself as Fleck, the brother of Flick. He had told Freyes about what Lilly and the Elders had found when they got to the Mystical Mountains. Lilly had sent a white Hare racing from the mountains, with Fleck hanging on in her long, hairy ear. Then, when the Hare had become exhausted, Fleck leaped onto a Fox who had taken him far across the pine forests until she could journey no more. Then Fleck caught a ride on a Water Rat and then flew on the shoulder of a Sparrow, which delivered him safely to the Kingdom of Dragonflies.

Fleck talked so fast that several times Freyes had to stop him and get him to start again. But, eventually, Freyes learned of the mysteries of the mountains and Lilly's incredible plan. But more importantly for now, Freyes learned that the dreaded dark Queen Eglarth had sent a swarm of giant hornets and they were heading straight for the Dragonfly Kingdom.

Freyes was, of course, told by Lilly before he and Leafel and Skeye left for home that they were to escort the fairies to the Dragonfly Kingdom, as the Fairy Kingdom was still in ruin and far too dangerous to stay there. So they had taken them to their own kingdom, where they hastily built shelters in the hollows of the giant old Oaks. There they waited, safe for now.

Then Freyes, who had taken up the mantle of Dragonfly King after the death of Vanos, got all the dragonflies together and told them of the cunning plan hatched by a little, unassuming black fairy.

"We will trust Lilly," he said, after some expressed concern.

"Yes, trust her we must," added Skeye.

"Never let us down, she has," added Leafel, still struggling with his words. "Not today, not even...yesterday and certainly not ever."

The other dragonflies nodded in agreement. Then Freyes had black dragonflies stationed at every entry to every hollow of every tree. Three hundred and thirty three black dragonflies, for three hundred and thirty-three fairy families. The black dragonflies, with their thick shells and stunning, shiny black eyes and white wings with black veins, were warrior dragonflies and very difficult to overcome in battle. When all was in readiness, the remaining dragonflies took up their positions, hiding in the reeds near the edge of the lakes which formed a boundary to their world. There they waited.

They waited for a day and a night and then another day, plus yet another night. But Lilly did not come. Freyes started to worry and lose faith that she ever would. But this time he kept that worry to himself, burying it behind a wall of trust.

Then, on the third morning, as the sun rose as it always had over the hills in the East and cast great long shadows across the forest floor and the waters of the lakes, a distant humming was heard over the chirping of birds, the croaking of frogs and the rustling of furry creatures.

Freyes looked towards the sky and saw what he imagined was a cloud gently crossing the path of the sun. *Strange*, he thought only to himself. *Such an unusually dark cloud for this time of day.* But when Skeye flew up on the command of Freyes to take a closer look, he returned with a report that made them all worry and fret.

The humming became louder, as if a great multitude of wings were beating together and Freyes realized what it was. He looked at his companions.

"They are here."

Inside the tree hollows, parents cradled the young in their arms and buried the little ones deep under their wings as the fairies also heard the terrible sound. Then the forest became dark again as the black mass of hornets appeared above them. Freyes, Skeye and Leafel watched as the mass descended, circling like a churning cloud right before a storm, closer and closer until they could see the fierce yellow eyes of the terrible hornets.

First one, then another landed in the middle of the dragonfly nests at the very heart of their kingdom. The hornets searched rapidly, desperately thrashing their huge bodies to the left and to the right. But when they discovered the nests were empty, they flew into a rage and tore the nests apart. Then they stopped and peered into the dark of the forests, turning their bodies, flicking their eyes about, watching for clues.

When they saw nothing but trees and shrubs and reeds, they spread their wings and with a thunderous noise, began lifting into the sky. For a moment, Freyes was convinced they were leaving, but when they stopped a little above the ground he knew it had been one hope too many, with only one small hope remaining.

Each one, moved forward, in a different direction than the others. Their bright yellow eyes searched like the light of flaming torches, casting beams about them. Small creatures darted off in fright when the light fell upon their skin. The swarm spread out and approached menacingly. Some towards the reeds, where the dragonflies were hiding and some towards the Oaks where the fairies were.

Freyes was beginning to panic, but he dare not move and neither did the others. The hornets were much larger then dragonflies, certainly much bigger than Freyes had imagined. When he saw the great yellow discs appear above the reeds nearby, he thought it was all about to end. But just when a hornet cast its eyes on him, there was a sudden flash of blue light that seemed to come from the direction of the middle of their kingdom. Instantly the hornet responded by flinging its dark body about and sped off in the direction of the explosion of light. Then there was another flash of brilliant light so powerful that Freyes had to shield his eyes. Then there was nothing. No humming, no buzzing, no sound in the forests or above the waters. Everything was still.

After a few moments, Freyes decided to fly up above the reeds. He wasn't sure of what had happened. But curiosity overcame him. As he took off, Leafel and Skeye and some of the others followed him. When he rose above the reeds and had a clear view of the kingdom, his eyes widened, but not with fear. When he realized what he was seeing, he darted off towards the nests.

Lilly stood in the middle of a patch of bare ground. Beside her stood the fairy elders, Daniith on one side and Sethbasish on the other. Daniith had his staff and Sethbasish had his spear. But Lilly held something in her hands that still glowed bright blue.

All around them, in every direction, strewn all about the kingdom, were the bodies of the hornets, legs everywhere, wings still, eyes now dim and lifeless. Freyes felt suddenly very guilty for having doubted Lilly. She said she would come, she had sent him a message.

"Don't worry my friend," said Lilly as she saw Freyes land and approach her with shame written in the way he walked and bowed his head low.

Daniith gave Lilly a nod and a wink and then both he and Sethbasish smiled. Then there was a roar of applause as the dragonflies buzzed their wings in excitement. The fairies, which had until that moment, been still hiding in the trees, came out, one family at a time and flew down to meet Lilly on the ground.

Lilly looked all about her. Some wore expressions of relief, some had tears of joy and the children, who must surely have been terrified, came out from under the wings of their parents and stepped cautiously towards Lilly.

"My family," said Lilly, with a beaming smile.

CHAPTER 11: THE BLUE TANZANITE CHARMS

"She will be angry when she comes," said Lilly to the elders and her trusted companions. "We defeated Denheroth at the foot of the mountains and not for the first time."

Lilly took off the necklace of blue charms she had been given. The Elders had asked her what they were, but there had been no time to explain until now.

"These charms I have been given carry all the magic from the memory of every fairy who has ever lived. My mother, my father, your mother and your father, your mother's mother and father since the very first fairy in the very first flower in the very first garden in our kingdom."

The Elders and the dragonflies watched intently the beautiful incandescent glow. Together with Lilly's own aura, which had grown brighter with every new power she possessed, made Lilly herself glow bright in the dark of the night, casting shadows of fairies and dragonflies against the great forest oaks about them.

The Elders did not ask Lilly how she used them. Neither did the dragonflies question her ability. She had defeated Denheroth again and he was no longer a threat. Now the only thing remaining, the only evil left in the entire world, was that of the Queen.

"The Queen is powerful, of that there can be little doubt. And she will use every trick, every dark spell, every charm to her advantage. She can destroy us. I alone have not the strength to overcome her."

When the Elders and the dragonflies heard this, doubt spread in their hearts as a flush of fear.

"I know your hearts. I feel your doubt. I hear that voice inside each of you, but never fear. For so long as we are together, the Elders, each with their own knowledge of magic, the dragonflies with their hearts as strong as their wings and all the hope of the fairies and every creature that lives and breathes in the world, we can overcome the Queen."

Lilly let her words soak deep into every heart. She spoke to them softly, but there was a certain power in her words, which cast a blanket of hope above them, which then enveloped their souls and made them believe her words.

"Tomorrow, in the evening, at midnight, the Queen intends to strike. And strike she will. But how she strikes and where is entirely up to us. She will come with her minions, she will come with her soldiers, the roaches, she will come at us with everything she has. But we will not stand in her way."

Dannith gave Sethbasish a confused look. The dragonflies started clicking and flicking their heads this way and then that. Lilly waited for them to settle.

"We don't need to do anything at all. We will let the Queen's own evil, her own power, her own rage destroy her for us. We only need one thing and it is something I have long avoided using and never wanted to use."

Again she stopped speaking, while the others allowed her words to form a shape, which showed them an image in their hearts and minds and that image was all she needed to convince them. Once each of them saw it, it was as if the sun appeared in the dark of night and one by one it dawned on them, that Lilly indeed was right.

"Deception."

"Yes, yes, deception is what she knows. It's what she understands," said Freyes.

"Deception, of course," added Skeye.

They looked at Leafel, expecting him to nod in agreement, but he was still mulling over what she had said first and was clearly struggling to keep up. Lilly was about to speak again, when finally Leafel interjected.

"Deceive the deceiver. Believe the believer. Weave with the weaver. Dream with the dreamer."

At first Freyes and Skeye did not know what to make of it. But Daniith in a moment of revelation, spoke for him in a way they would understand.

"I could not have put it better myself Leafel," he said, smiling.

Leafel was on a roll and could not stop thinking out loud. "If the Queen is the deceiver then we are the believers. I believe in the believer, yes, that's right, the believer. Lilly is the dreamer of dreams. Dreams she had, lots of dreams, each one true. Each one correct and utterly true. The believers must believe and the deceiver must deceive, but only believers can deceive a deceiver."

They all stood staring at Leafel, as if he wasn't a simple dragonfly, but some sage or mystic or wise old hermit who had just returned after a long absence. Then Lilly stepped towards him.

"My friend, you are the only one who does not have a staff or even a pound of magic. You are not gifted with words or insight and yet you have just proved to be the most knowledgeable and gifted of all dragonflies. Your simple logic has expressed in your own way and with your own words the obvious in a way few would ever dream of being witty enough to say."

If he had been a proud creature, Leafel would surely have lifted his head above the others, wiped his crown with a foot and strutted about pompously, but he was the most humble of all creatures and was clearly still trying to figure out if what he had just said was even correct. Lilly climbed up onto his shoulders and patted him gently on his head.

"If we are to deceive the Dark Queen Eglarth, then we had better be ready when she comes. But for now each to his or her own home to rest, for tomorrow we ready for the mightiest of battles."

Before Lilly retired to a tree, she found Fleck, the brother of Flick. Flick she had sent to the dungeons of the Queen and she now told Fleck why.

Your brother is on a mission. In the morning you will see what that mission was. Fleck jumped up onto her shoulder after she spoke to him and she flew up into the tree. And there, as she closed her eyes to sleep, Lilly did not dream a single dream for the first time in a very long time.

Paul G Day

CHAPTER 12: THE WRATH OF THE DARK QUEEN

When Fleck woke up early, the light of dawn had not yet come. He was excited by what Lilly had said to him the night before and he watched from the opening of her hollow as the first light crept ever so slowly over the Eastern Sky. When the sun finally peeked its rosy face above the hills, he jumped down from the tree and found a squirrel hunting for acorns. He jumped up and whispered in the squirrel's ear and it ran off and climbed the tallest tree in the whole forest.

There, from his vantage point high up on the highest branch, Fleck could see almost the whole world spread out beneath him. And there he waited.

Lilly woke to the sound of excited voices from below and flew down from her tree to meet with the Elders and dragonflies and fairies starting to gather. They had all heard it, a thumping, like the sound of hundreds of feet all running at once. At first Daniith was concerned, but when he saw Lilly smiling his concern gave way to anticipation.

The sound grew louder and louder until fairies and dragonflies started backing up towards the trees again. Suddenly first one creature and then another leaped out from the bushes and reeds.

A rabbit, then a hare, then foxes, squirrels, rats and all manner of furry creatures. They bounded towards the gathering. Lilly stepped forward and held up a hand and the creatures stopped in front of her. Sethbasish and Daniith breathed a sigh of relief, fearing they would be overrun with animals and stampeded to death had they not stopped.

A squirrel scampered down a nearby tree and ran over to the creatures and stopped. After a little while two voices spoke into Lilly's ear. One of them was Flick and the other his brother.

"Are these the minions from the dungeon?" asked Daniith, a little confused.

"They were," answered Lilly. "Now no longer."

Again she heard a little voice explain to her.

"I am told by Flick that as soon as he freed them from imprisonment, the Queen became enraged and chased after them. But her errant magic missed its intended target and as soon as the minions were far away from her clutches, they began to change and the curse was lifted. So, by the time they reached us, they became as they once were."

"Now the Queen will be doubly mad, if that were even possible," said Freyes.

"Yes, doubly mad and will double her efforts," added Skeye.

"She will stop at nothing." Said Daniith and then nodded at Lilly, who merely brushed away their concern with a beaming smile.

"We have little time. Gather everyone together, we are leaving for the Fairy Kingdom.

Each one carried what they could on the backs of the dragonflies. And after flying until the sun was at its highest in the sky, they came upon a sight that Lilly well remembered. The last time she had been here, the fairy kingdom had been devastated. The homes were destroyed. The flowers had died and not a creature could be seen anywhere.

They flew down and landed on a patch of ground in the middle of what should have been their kingdom. Around them everything was barren and wasted. Only the slender trunks of the trees remained.

But the fairies and the dragonflies and all the furry creatures, wasted no time. They had brought with them flowers and reeds and bark and sticks and colorful seeds and acorn shells full of water. They unloaded it all from the backs of the dragonflies and set about their work. Then Lilly told Flick to gather all the fleas from all the creatures with feathers and fur and explain to them the very special job she had for them. So the creatures of the forest took off in all directions, returning with crystals they had gathered from streams, between rocks, in gullies and in sand.

Then Lilly ordered the crystals to be fastened together and fashioned into large reflective tablets. These were placed behind the flowers which were meant to resemble the fresh new homes of fairies.

Then, after many long hours, just before the sun started settling over the Western hills, they all stood back and looked at what they had done.

"It looks the same. Indeed exactly the same as before," remarked Sethbasish.

"Indeed it does," added Daniith.

"Yes, exactly. Exactly the same...the same as what, exactly?" said Leafel, returning to the same way he always spoke when he appeared confused. The others could not help but laugh, not because he was silly, but because he was right, even if he didn't know it himself.

"The same except for these," said Freyes, holding up the last woven crystal tablet. Then he placed the tablet behind a large flower and made sure that's where it would stay.

"Now all we need to do is ask for volunteers." This was the part of her plan she was most concerned about. In order to deceive the Queen, she had to make sure the fairies understood what that meant. She looked at each of them and decided it was too much to ask of mothers and little ones and fathers still with young families. "But only those who have the least to lose can volunteer. Any fairy with a family or not yet named or not yet of age must go with the others back to the dragonfly kingdom."

She did not have to wait long for answers.

"I will volunteer," said one young fairy boy stepping courageously forward. Then another joined him, followed by an elderly fairy, then even more joined them until fifty fairies stood in a circle about Lilly.

She looked at them all and decided that even though less in number than she had planned, it would have to do. She sent all the dragonflies back with the rest of the fairies and the creatures who were rescued from the dungeons of the Queen. Only Freyes and Leafel and Skeye and Daniith and Sethbasish and six more Elders remained behind, adding their number to the fifty volunteers.

Lilly stood and regarded each of them for a moment. To anyone looking at her from the outside, they would not say she was the same creature who left the kingdom so long ago in her quest to find the fairies. She was then still only a child. Now she was more than even she could have imagined.

"I cannot tell you how risky this is. All the power of all the fairies of all the ages cannot prepare us for what we must face tonight. Despite everything I have seen and learned and done, I fear it might not be enough and if we fail, we will lose everything. The world as we know it will change forever and we cannot let that happen."

Any joy on the faces of those who were gathered was washed away by what Lilly said. Only solemn looks, flushed with the realization that this could all be for nothing, was plainly visible on each and every face.

"But," Lilly continued before they began to lose hope altogether. "Daniith has the Staff of Ages. Freyes has the Staff of Vanos. Sethbasish has the Spear of Knowing and I have the Charms of Truth. And if that is not enough to overcome the Queen, we have one more surprise for her and that is the Gathering of Deception, of which all you are now a part."

Again she allowed the words to seep into their hearts. Again she spoke to their inner souls. She had learned this last skill from the creatures of the mountains. Every time she used it their souls became more and more transparent and their hearts became more and more known to her. She could even hear the whispers of doubt and fear spoken so softly in their minds, that it took all her power to hear them.

"We are all that is left between the world we know and love and the world the Queen would bring upon us all. Each one of you plays a part in this last act. Each one of you has a song to write when this is done. What that song is, depends on what sound the music in your heart now makes. So, make music in your hearts, make it sure and strong. Have all the heavens sing along. Lift up your heads, raise up your hearts, feel the warmth of my own heart as I breath it to you."

As she said this Lilly started glowing a vibrant orange, which spread out from her and touched everyone. When it did they were filled with her courage. Then they sang a song. The same song they sang when they first knew she had come to rescue them in the dungeon and the sound of it filled the air. A chorus of beauty, echoing off the trees. It made its way out from that place and even reached the ears of the distant fairies now settled in the kingdom of dragonflies.

Then, long after the sun had disappeared and well into the ever darkening night, they settled into their positions, each fairy on a flower. The dragonflies, Freyes, Skeye and Leafel, hid in the bushes a little way off. They were joined by Lilly, Daniith and Sethbasish. The remaining Elders also lay down in their own flowers.

There they all waited. The flames of a camp fire flickered in the middle of the kingdom. Its' light made the shadows of the flowers dance amongst the timbers of the forest, like the shadows of souls awaiting the day they will live again.

Finally, at almost midnight, a sound was heard in the distance. It was preceded by a strange pink glow, which crept closer and closer to the kingdom of fairies. The sound was like a mistress singing her sweet lullaby in the cool night air, intended to seduce whomever heard it into believing that naught but the gentlest of souls walked nearby.

Lilly and the others watched intently as the figure of a familiar presence cast shadows hued with pink throughout the timbers of the trees. Then, the Dark Queen appeared between the trees, her red eyes now glowing brighter than ever before, her dark wings spread out wide and high. She was cloaked in a dark cloud that hissed and cracked whenever it came into contact with anything. She appeared to float above the forest floor. In times past Lilly herself would have been paralyzed with fear. But this was exactly what she expected.

"Lilly, oh my sweet Lilly," the queen echoed through the forest in a voice like that of Lilly's mother. But Lilly was not fooled. She had to tone down her glow and it took most of her concentration to do so. She did not want to be discovered too soon.

"My sweet dear little one. Don't be afraid. A truce, a truce is all I want. Yes, a truce is all I am after. We can live as one you and I. So similar we are, with our dark skin and our familiar hearts." The magic of the Queen's charms were almost overpowering to all but the strongest of hearts. But Lilly had been deceived once before by the charms of the Queen and never again.

So hidden she remained until the perfect time, which just happened to be when the Queen was within eyesight of the village.

"So, you have worked your magic and rebuilt your kingdom. How sweet." Eglarth's red eyes narrowed and then she looked up. Suddenly there was the sound of Eagles screeching high above, which was something Lilly had not anticipated. The Eagles circled a few times and then dived down and, to Lilly's dismay looked as if they might land in the middle of the village and ruin all her plans.

They did not. Instead, they came to rest high up in the trees. If they had landed, Lilly feared she would not reach the fairies in time and the large bodies of the Eagles might dislodge the crystal tablets.

"You see I have brought friends. You remember Lilly, don't you? You followed them into the bowels of the underworld. So long ago. Yes an age it seems. That's where you met Denheroth. Remember? You vanquished him not once, but TWICE!" She shouted that last word so loud it was like a crack of thunder which made the trees shake. The fire in the middle of the village almost went out, but it sprang back to life when she softened her tone again.

"You must be nearby, my precious little Lilly. Yes, so near, so very near." Suddenly the Queen turned her head and looked right at Lilly. Lilly wasted no time. She clutched the charms, spoke the words and they exploded into life, sending the Queen and her Roaches toppling backwards.

Lilly, Daniith, Sethbasish and the three dragonflies took off to the middle of the fairy village and stopped. The Queen got back up and brushed herself off and then rushed quickly towards them. She wore a fierce expression and let out a scream of hatred. Again Lilly clutched the charms and there was a second explosion, but this time the Queen was ready for it and she held up her charms to repel it. The force of it almost knocked Lilly and her companions over and would have blown away the flowers if Lilly had not been quick enough to use the charms. The Queen put all her magic behind her force as pink beams of powerful light struck at Lilly. Blue beams of light came from her own charms, forcing the pink back, but not enough. While she held the Queen at bay, she spoke over her shoulder.

"Get ready." She hoped the others heard her. If she was to deceive the Queen, she had to make it seem as if she was able to withstand, but not too long. Lilly allowed the power of the Queen to overcome her and when she felt ready, she released her grip and the pink beams thrust her to the ground, along with the others.

The Queen approached her menacingly, focused almost entirely on Lilly. "Did you think that your weak little powers were a match for me?" By this time the fairies had stood up in their flowers, as they had been told to do. "Oh, how quaint. All the little darlings are back in their little homes. How fitting that they should die where they stand.

The Queen's eyes narrowed to just red slits as she leant forward and extended her staff outwards. The dark crystal started glowing pink.

"You took my minions. You killed Denheroth. You managed to turn the entire world against me, my...little...dark...angel." She said through gritted teeth. Then Eglarth raised herself up again and pulled the staff back. The pink light became a ball of energy which sparkled and cracked and pulsated in front of them. "Well, as we all know, black angels belong in a dark place."

Just before the Queen went to strike, Lilly clutched the charms one last time. A shield went up in front of her and her companions just as the pink beams struck it. Lilly managed to hold it back for just long enough.

"NOW!" she yelled and this time her voice was like thunder. The Queen's eyes widened in surprise, but she kept the beams pointed at Lilly. By this time the fairies had ducked behind the crystal tablets, holding onto them at the sides on the frames of woven reed. Off to her left Daniith struck from his staff and caught the

Queen off balance slightly, but it was not
enough. Sethbasish held his spear outstretched
in a feeble attempt to protect Lilly. Lilly glanced
to her left and right. The Queen let out a howl
of rage because she was not yet overcoming
Lilly. She uttered something devilishly loud and
a second beam struck Lilly's shield. Lilly fell
backwards and the beams of light thrust
against one of the crystal tablets, which then
sent beams of light sideways, connecting with
other crystal tablets, until a ring of pink light
encircled the Queen.

"What new magic is this? I've been deceived."

Lilly got to her feet and held up the blue
charms so that the largest charm was in her
hands. Instantly the fairy behind Lilly aimed at
the charm and a burst of pink light mixed with
blue shot a powerful beam directly at the staff
of the Queen. Her staff splintered and then
shattered into a thousand pieces. The Queen
raised her wings in rage in a vain effort to
shield herself, but she was too late. The beam
shot through her chest and the shock of it sent
blue and pink lightning all through her body,
burning her skin and setting her clothing and
wings alight. She let out one last howl, but this

time it was the dying howl of a mad Queen. The Eagles, who had seen the whole thing, Panicked and took off from the trees, screeching into the night.

Silence once more returned to the forest. The body of the Queen lay smoldering in smoky ruin. Lilly herself had used up most of her energy and lay flat on the ground. Daniith and Sethbasish rushed to her side and lifted her up. She was joined by the other fairies.

When she was finally able to stand on her own, she stepped over to the massive body of the Queen who now lay strangely lifeless and silent. Lilly had not allowed herself to dream of this day. She did not like the feeling that came with deception, nor the feeling that accompanied taking the life of a creature, any creature, even an evil Queen. Yet, she had done what she had promised to do. She had rid the world of evil once and now for all.

The Elders stood silently next to her, as did Freyes, Leafel and Skeye. Then, after a few moments of thought, they left the body of the Queen to the fate of a long, undignified decay and headed back to the Dragonfly Kingdom once more. But as Lilly left, she glanced up at the ruined village, now tainted with the impact of evil, permanently scared and burning around the edges. *If there is a casualty in all of this*, she thought, *it must surely be innocence.*

With that final thought, Lilly turned and mounted her faithful Freyes and was joined soon after by the Elder Daniith. The others mounted Leafel and Skeye, all fifty of them, plus the elders, on the backs of these magnificent insects, the dragonflies.

EPILOGUE: SOMETHING SO VERY RARE

The Queen was still finding it hard to get used to her new role. She had been humbled by her coronation. An endless stream of creatures from all over the world visited her in her new home not all that far from the Dragonfly Kingdom. Her fame had spread to the mountains, to the rivers and to the coasts and even found its way to the peoples of the islands far off.

So dark and yet so beautiful she was, adorned with wondrous cloths made of rarest and finest materials. Even her Majesty Queen Sheebas came to greet her and bowed low before her throne. The Frog Lords of Sereth-Eben knelt before her too and finally the creatures of the mystical mountains, who never left their home in the snow, making this one exception to visit the new Queen of all the world.

Her day was filled with activity and special events for much of the time in her reign, but at night, when she was alone, Lilly thought only of her parents.

"They would be proud," said Daniith late one evening. "So very proud of you, my precious,

dear, sweet Lilly. Queen Lilly Black De-Small the First. Such a rare gift to be honored in such a way, especially for one still so very small. Something strange and yet, so very rare indeed."

As time passed and Lilly came fully into her own, the time came for her to choose the future father of her offspring. Having seen that he resembled her own father in so many ways, Lilly settled on a fairy named Leith. The dragonflies gave him a new name, Leithal White De-Fine on account of his pale features and all agreed it was the perfect match.

It was not very much longer after this, that together Leith and Lilly took a child from their own flower and nobody was surprised at all that it was as dark as Lilly herself. Leith presented the child to the Elders and this time, they did not hesitate to name her:

Jasmine Black De-Small.

ABOUT THE AUTHOR

Paul G Day studied Children's Literature, Young Adult Fiction, Writing for Children, English and the Dramatic Arts at Flinders University. He has a Bachelor of Arts and a Post Graduate Degree in Education specializing in English and Drama. As a Teacher, one of 9 children himself and with two grown children, Paul knows a thing or two about children. He has written thousands of poems, short stories and other written works, specializing in Children's Writing. Paul has several self-published books to his credit including 4 books of poems, 4 children's books and now 3 novels. He loves to write for children and his stories draw on real life experiences for inspiration.

OTHER BOOKS BY THIS AUTHOR

STAR CHILD SERIES
Book 1: Star Child: The Cosmic Birth
Book 2: Star Child: Daughter of Destiny
Book 3: Star Child: The Sons of Earth

YOUNG ADULT FICTION
The Black Fairy and the Dragonfly
Escape From The Dark Queen
Kipp The Copper Coast Kid

CHILDREN'S FICTION
Lucky and Scratch
The Misadventures of Red Bear
The Fairies of Muddy Glen
Monkey's ABC Alphabet and Animals
The Magic Fairies ABC123

POETRY ANTHOLOGIES
When Comes Darkness
Children of Heaven
Glass House

WEBSITES AND BLOGS
My Blog
http://redbearbooks.wordpress.com/
Amazon Author Page
http://www.amazon.com/-/e/B007QGRJPU
Twitter Page
https://twitter.com/RedBearBooks
Email
Paulday98@yahoo.com

Made in the USA
Lexington, KY
02 July 2019